Come Fly with Captain Kangaroo

Illustrated by
Mandy Foot

LOTHIAN
Children's Books

For brilliant books, fun and games visit

www.mandyfoot.com.au

My friends and family are flying with Captain Kangaroo. How many of us can you count in each picture?

FOR JOSHY AND POPS

A Lothian Children's Book

Published in Australia and New Zealand in 2011
by Hachette Australia
Level 17, 207 Kent Street, Sydney NSW 2000
www.hachettechildrens.com.au

10 9

Text copyright © Hachette Australia 2011
Illustrations copyright © Mandy Foot 2011

National Library of Australia
Cataloguing-in-Publication data

Mandy Foot.
Come fly with Captain Kangaroo / Mandy Foot.

978 0 7344 1194 5 (pbk.)

For children.

A823.4

Designed by Kinart Pty Ltd
Colour reproduction by Splitting Image
Printed in China by Toppan Leefung Printing Limited

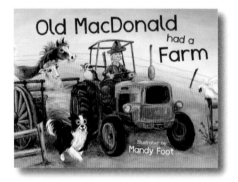

Australia is a **giant** land from the outback to the sea.
Aussies love to travel and sky high's the way to be!

It's early in the morning, and there's so much to do.
Who's arriving at the airport? It's Captain Kangaroo!

The check-in desk is busy at any time of day.
There are tickets to be printed and **heavy bags** to weigh.

The crew are LOADING UP THE LUGGAGE and packing up the meals.
They're inspecting wings and engines, the fuel tank and the wheels.

The attendants are all SMILING, standing ready at the doors.
The passengers are lining up. They can't wait to get on board.

Doors have closed for take-off.
Seatbelts go **click - clack**.

Life jackets are below your seats,
safety exits front and back.

The captain taxis down the runway, slowly and with care.
He checks in with the control tower, then SOARS UP IN THE AIR.

It's **bumpy** flying into clouds but at last we're through.
Lean against the windows. You don't want to miss this view!

The sandwiches and lamingtons
are a welcome sight.

There's something about FLYING
that brings on an appetite.

Tables folded, **SEATS** UPRIGHT. Hasn't it been fun?
Now it's time for landing. Our journey's almost done.

Thump! Thump! go the wheels
as the captain lands the plane.
'Welcome home!' he tells the passengers.
'Come fly with us again!'